THE
TAIL-LESS
COW

DR. (MRS) NGOZI ANCHOR-LEE OKORO

Copyright © 2021

DR. (MRS) NGOZI ANCHOR-LEE OKORO

DEDICATION

To the Holy Trinity for loving me, saving me and comforting me in times of distress. My God, my father, my savior and my greatest teacher; by your grace I will forever be grateful for a dream come true and for enjoying your presence.

ACKNOWLEDGMENTS

I am still indebted to the Holy Trinity for the saving and sustaining grace.

I am not ungrateful to my own husband, Mr Kenneth Onyebuchi and children: Chinaemerem, Ifeanyichukwu, Anaetochukwu, Akachukwu, Kosisochukwu and Chisom, the baby of the house for their all round support and useful distractions.

I owe a million thanks to Sir Chris Anunihu, Dr, Stephen Ejiogu, the Medical Director, Chisom Hospital and Maternity Orlu, the entire Okoro-Ehirim's family, the Ugorji's family, Inyama's family and the Opara's family of Obeama Nguru Mbaise.

My special thanks goes to all my spiritual fathers, past and present for nurturing and maturing me in the faith especially Bishop G.U. Ukanwa, Bishop Chris Odoemena, Pastor Obinna Ekwueme, Revd. Vitalis Anaele- Ugoji, Revd. Sam Ajare, Revd.

Sam Daniels, Bro and Sis Mauren Onyema, Pastor Nwokeji, Pastor Okoro, Jehoshapat, Pastor Emma Okoro (S.O.), Pastor Victor C. Ekechukwu and Pastor W.F. Kumuyi for stirring the gift of God in me.

I will never forget my mentor Dr. (Mrs) A.C. Izuagba and Dr. Charles Ugwegbulam who God used to bring me to the academic limelight.

Prof. Onuekwuesi, J.A., Revd. Dr Bethel Azubuike, Pastor Gerald Okere, Pastor Lekwuwa, E., Prof, and Dr. (Mrs) Kenneth Nnadi, Prof. Christopher Dike and Mrs Idih, C.N for their moral and financial support.

It will tantamount to ingratitude if I fail to acknowledge all my lecturers and erudite scholars during my doctoral degree programme especially my supervisor Prof. David Eka, of the blessed memory. Prof. Ashong, Prof. Inyang Udofot, Dr. Friday Okon, Dr Josiah Obong. Prof. Ushie and Pastor Ezekiel Udom all your invaluable contributions towards my advancement in the world of academics.

ABOUT THE BOOK

Fictionalization is one way of capturing true life experiences for didactic benefits of the readers. Yet, such true stories are concealed with literary ornaments. This piece is highly recommended for those who are losing faith , those facing challenges, those who need encouragements, as well as those who need entertainment. The author's foray into literary writing is part of her untapped God-given talents having focused more of her scholarly energy on linguistic and educational concerns. Part who draws inspiration from Ada as the story flows round her struggles, climaxing at her success against all odds.

Dr Smart Chibuike Mbarachi

THE AUTHOR'S NOTE

The tail-less cow is an admixture of creativity and reality. It is a fiction. It is a product of the author's reminiscences about life and its vicissitudes. The entire story revolves around Ada, the central character who exhibited a strong passion and will to break away from mediocrity and sorry-situation.

In the society, there are people like Ada because no writer writes in a vacuum. People like Ada in the novel would like to take the bull by the horn despite all odds. For such people, they are focused and will not allow distractions on their way to achieving greater heights. That is to say not careful about the company they keep, may not reach their destination or accomplish their dreams. You can see that truly, life is a journey, a book and a teacher. Until we come to the end of life, we keep moving, we keep reading and we keep learning.

It is said "Destiny" can be delayed, but it cannot be denied". Yet, you must dare like Daniel to accomplish your goals in life. My sincere admonition for every reader as a wife or mother is that "mothers should endeavor to play their God-given role in the family to be able to win their husbands, enjoy love, peace, unity and progress in their homes.

As a teacher, let teacher ensure that they are role-models, knowledgeable, wise, self-disciplined and God-fearing because nobody gives what he or she does not have. As a student, it pays to be single-minded and maintain good communication.

As a born again-to succeed here and hereafter, Christian experiences are genuine and current. As a carrer woman- I want to tell "Be strong in the Lord", "where there is a will, there is a way". Life is "what you sow, you reap".

CHAPTER ONE

Reminiscences

It all started like a dream. For Ada, she wanted to be a graduate in life. But you see, there are two sides to a coin. Luck plays a lucky role in nature, so does lack of luck. Some people are born great, others achieve greatness. Life is a journey. It is full of riddles. It is like a shadow. It appears from end and disappears at the other end. Life is like kingdoms. For some, they blossom and wane suddenly. For some others, they take time to blossom. *"As you make your bed, so you lie on it,"* is true to life and that reminds us of the nature-nurture controversy.

Don't forget the law of retributive justice. Remember that what happens in between life and death is a product of choice. Some people desire good things in life, but they are not willing to pay the price. Whereas, others cut corners with the hope of reaping where they did not sow. Many others lose sight of what the sages say "Suffer before pleasure", or as one Igbo adage puts it "Aka aja-aja n'ebute onu mmanu mmanu".

Never forget that life is too short and too precious for reckless rides. A reckless life is synonymous with manoeuvring to overtake between two moving vehicles on the busy highway. Some people, like the prodigal son, maybe fortunate to survive "near misses, but others might not be that lucky.

"Look before you leap is a warning sign post to recklessness" Ada will ever remember the words of her grandma. Think of events and developments surrounding your past. Can you smile or frown at some oddities that you are responsible for? It can be terrible to discover that you are the architect of your own misfortune.

But, it is not over, until it is over. Where there is a will, there is a way. Shall someone be grateful or curse the day of meeting you? Think twice, if your life has been a blessing or otherwise. "Success has many friends, but failure is an orphan". Keep your dream alive, her conscience would constantly remind her.

CHAPTER TWO

As her name implies, she is the first daughter and coincidentally the first child of Mr and Mrs Fred of Umualaoma. She has three siblings: Kemjika, Ikem and Nnedinma. Her father was a railway worker at Zaria, Northern Nigeria before the civil war. Her mother Nma was a complete house wife who engaged in petty trading. Her father was an only son of Pa Steve and wife. His elder sister Mama Janet married at Akuma. She was instrumental to getting Nma as a wife for her only brother. Nma's reputable family background attracted many suitors both far and near. She was a paragon of beauty, tall, elegant, fair in complexion, slim-fit with pointed nose and endowed with long hair that endeared her to all those who have eyes for aesthetics. She came from a prominent family in Ezuma in Akuma, the Aros in diaspora. She stopped her secondary education halfway and married before her elder sister Ukachi not just for the impending civil war, but because had no passion for education.

Nma was fortunate to have given birth to Ada and a son, Kemjika in quick succession before the war drove them back from Zaria. Indeed, she was a blessing to her parents. During the war many people died of hunger and kwashiorkor in addition to bombs and bullets. Kwashiorkor was a terrible disease as a result of malnutrition owing to scarcity of food. The effect of the civil war was so biting that people adopted various survival strategies. These strategies include; eating lizard as the highest meat available, cassava leaves as vegetable, fresh cassava tubers as ready meals among others. Ada refused to die as a result of Kwashiorkor but narrowly escaped death one of the days a fighter plane released a bomb in their bunker where they were taking refuge. It was through divine intervention that she sustained only an injury on the right side of her head towards her right ear. Her father quickly gave her first aid treatments, gathered compost leaves rubbed them together in his palms and applied the water as first aid on the bleeding part of her head. To some people, that would have marked their end of existence on this planet earth. In those days, many mothers willingly abandoned their children by the roadsides either because of excess luggage they were carrying or the incessant cry of such children in their bid to survive the ordeals of the war. Kudos to Red Cross Society that brought relieve materials such as powdered milk, corn meal, Quaker oat, egg yolk powder, drugs among others. These helped to save many lives including those abandoned children.

CHAPTER THREE

Life has its own vicissitudes and so is child upbringing. Ada's early childhood experiences cannot be fully documented without reference to her maternal home. Her Grandpa, Mazi as he was fondly called was a seasoned tailor. He was both famous and wealthy in substance among his contemporaries. In fact, story has it that the Ezuma's were the first people to build zinc house within their community and locality in the early 50s. Her maternal uncle Barr Olisakwe was a renowned lawyer with a family of five boys and a girl. He worked with the British council in the then East Central State, Enugu to be precise.

Mama Alice, popularly addressed as Mrs Mazi was an epitome of a virtuous woman. She was among the women who were trained in the art of home-making by the Whitemen under the auspices of the church. Nma had two sisters, auntie Nancy who married earlier and auntie Ukachi who married later. Unlike Nma, auntie Ukachi was a lover of education so she persevered and completed her Teachers' Training College (TTC) education after the war. That earned her an enviable position among her contemporaries. As a teacher in a University staff school, she got married to a good husband, a chartered accountant, and was blessed with three boys and a girl, all graduates.

For Mr Fred to make ends meet after the war, he secured another job with the Ministry of Agriculture as an Agric. extension officer in the small holder department in the State capital while his wife took to petty trading hence she had no certificate that would earn her a white collar job. However, there is something in a name. The semantic import of names predicates that parents should endeavour to give their children names that depict virtues and godliness. Ada's other names typified faith in God, blessing and courage.

"Train up a child in a way he should go
and when he is old, he will not depart
from it" **Proverbs 22:6**).

CHAPTER FOUR

Mama Alice herself, would always sing and read her Bible daily in spite of her old age. Some of her favourite songs that one can draw inspirations from are:

> *Aha Jisos di oke uto*
> *Na nti onye kwere*
> *O nakasi ya n'ahuhu*
> *N'achupu egwu ya*

> *How Sweet the name*
> *of Jesus sounds,*
> *To a believer's ear,*
> *and*
> *He gives him comfort*
> *in trouble and*
> *Drives away his*
> *fears.*

Ada grew under the tutelage of her maternal

grandma, who inculcated in her such virtues as love, generosity, fear of God, unity of purpose, self-confidence, self-discipline, respect for elders, honesty, selflessness, hard-work, and faith in God's unfailing promises. Her grandma was so generous and hardly would allow anybody that came her way to go without been fed. She would always have a portion of food reserved for visitors. As early in life as possible, Ada has started singing in the choir, participating in Igbo Bible reading. The act of Bible reading is imbibed during Sunday school and special occasions in the church. She imbibed the culture of hard-work as her grandma would always go to farm with her and her cousins.

On one occasion, they went to farm and were coming back late, Ada displayed childishness and naivety of heart "would you raise your leg, please it is becoming late" said her grandma implying to double her steps by walking fast. She stood at a place, raising her leg until her grandma who had gone far dictated that Ada was not responding to her conversation. But when she looked back and saw her standing still with one leg raised up, she shouted *"Kamalu ozuzu mapia kwa gi anya ma ya amapiakwala gi"*. She queried her for standing still seeing that the birds had already started singing. Ada replied "Akwa gi sim welie ukwum elu". The Grandma laughed "chei!" "onye futara uwa nwata gburie ewu". This means that one should celebrate ones success over ones childhood challenges.

CHAPTER FIVE

azi Okoronkwo who was popularly known as "Kabaka" was instrumental to inculcating good morals and cultural values in children. He was doing that during moonlights using folktales. Ada and her contemporaries would gather around Kabaka to listen to folktales while plucking his gray hair. Kabaka would in turn give them "Kai-Kai" the local hot drink in compensation for removing itching gray hairs on his head. He would also ask them questions based on the stories he told them in order to test their intelligence, aural-oral skills and their ability to take turns. This is because if anyone answers in a haste a question meant for someone else, the person would be reprimanded.

One of those stories told by Kabaka was the story of **"Unu dum"**, which is translated in English as "All of you". In that story, the major character, the tortoise who typified a fraudster due to famine, summoned all the birds and sold an idea to them.

He suggested that they would take a trip to the sky where he perceived there was abundance of food by setting some ground rules. First, they would lend him feathers individually. Second, that they would assume new names because those people living in the sky might not be conversant with their original or local names. All the birds bought the idea and did as the tortoise suggested. He was the last to take a new name and he chose "All of you".

Unfortunately, when they got to the sky, the story changed as the tortoise dominated the scenario, ate all and drank all that were presented to all of them because he would ask them when they dropped the food, drink and other delicacies "For who were these things meant for?" They would reply, "It is for all of you". That made the tortoise to eat and drink alone all that was presented for them. The reaction of all the birds became disastrous to the tortoise as each bird plucked their feathers in anger and left. When the tortoise asked the other birds to tell his wife "Alia" to bring out all their foams and other soft items in the home so that he could land safely from the sky, contrariwise, all the birds gave his wife the opposite of his request. So the wife instead of bringing out all the soft items in the house, she brought out all the weapon sat home. So the tortoise assumed his message was well delivered and so he land crashed.

The aftermath of that greed and selfishness was the patched shell of the tortoise. Another story was the *"Ahia Uya"* meaning "The *Uya* market" This was another scenario where the tortoise exhibited greed and craftiness, but was caught up in the web. Kabaka the narrator would start thus: Once upon a time! Time!! Time!!! There was famine in the land of the animals to the point that many prominent animals started dying of hunger. The tortoise devised a survival strategy by feigning to be the "Chief of the spirits" or "Ezemuo" in Igbo. So on the market days, he brought out his "Oji", an iron digger, decorated with beads, feathers and other metals then proceeded to the market square. The people in the market would take to their heels. They abandoned all their goods and property and escaped for their dear lives at the noise of the "Oji" and his spirit-like chanting thus:

Ahia uya sue-sue uyaa, Uya mbele uya
2x
Agwada kuwa onwe ya, uyaa uya mbele
uya
Egbe gbawa onwe ya, uyaa uya mbele
uya 3x

The tortoise did that successfully on two market days, but before the next market day, all the sages in that town hazarded a solution to that problem. It is said that everyday is for the thief, but one day is for the owner of the house. They brought a doll-baby (toy)at the centre of the market decorated with "erontuochi" that was masking the doll baby with a permanent smiling face and a goat meat leg in its hand all glued together.

On the D-day, when the tortoise came and saw nobody in the market except the doll baby in the centre of the market, he went closer to the baby and was begging for a share of the meat. After much pleading, the doll baby was still beaming with smiles. The tortoise got annoyed and threatened to slap her if she would not give him some part of that meat. As if in real life, the baby was still smiling and the tortoise slapped her in anger for failing to grant his request and his hand got stuck. Eventually the tortoise started pleading for mercy yet the doll baby was still beaming with smiles.

When she could not release him, he got infuriated the more and gave her a nod, hit her with the leg and was hanging in front of her until the villagers gathered around to see the monster that has been terrorizing them. You can guess, what do you think the villagers would do to the tortoise for all his atrocities? From these stories, Kabaka used the tortoise to discourage children from vices such as laziness, greed, dishonesty and selfishness and in turn inculcate in them team spirit, hard-work, honesty, respect for cultural values, love, dignity of labour and selflessness.

CHAPTER SIX

As the sages say, "never despise the days of little beginning". In the early seventies (70s), Ada started her primary education at central school Ede, which was interrupted by her journey to her maternal home – Akuma. There, she started her primary education afresh while living with her maternal grandmother. She was almost discouraged because each time she went to school Mr Obiyo her class teacher would ask her to go back home until her hand would touch her ear. Ada would cry and refuse to go home at such instances because she loved education. That situation was possible because nursery education was not popular then. Later, Ada enrolled and exhibited brilliant performances as it is said that learning goes with age. On two occasions, she was withdrawn from school and her education was truncated as a result of baby-sitting. That was between 1973 and 1975. She was ridiculed by some of her mates who overtook her as a result of baby-sitting. When she eventually resumed school due to her excellent performances, her uncle Barr Olisakwe, who came back from Coal city and saw the potentials in her; decided to take her to the city with the hope of training her up to the university level. And that would be in one of the famous, prestigious universities in the country. When Ada received the news, instead of being excited, she had mixed feelings because of the fear of parting with her family members and especially her younger siblings.

Beforehand, she has developed an unfeigned love for her siblings, right from childhood. One day as she was coming back from school and saw Kemjika, her immediate younger brother's eye swollen; she could not wait to find out the cause, rather threw her slate away and wept soar, refused to eat and be comforted. She was afraid that her brother has lost his eye.

The grandma also encouraged her to follow her uncle to the city in order to accomplish her dream and love for qualitative education. Sooner or later, Ada's fear was confirmed immediately they got to the city. Her uncle, a legal practitioner and a university staff took her to a Reverend Sister in the campus as a house help.

She passed through bitter experiences in the hands of the so-called Reverend Sister who was as wicked as Jezebel. She would flog Ada mercilessly or ask her to kneel down for hours. At times, the Sister would ask her to wash her white robes, the university bedding which was too difficult for her to wash given her age at that time. As soon as Ada realised that she was at the wrong place and not only that, the qualitative education her uncle promised her was a mirage, she concluded that her uncle has given her false hope. Although, taking her to the city according to her uncle was also a way of alleviating the burden of her mother, she made up her mind to go back to her root and that without delay. When her uncle learnt about her insistence to go back, he became angry with her decision but had no better option than to take her back home. She could not stop crying day and night *"kpolaa moo, kpolaa moo"*(take me back, take me back) each time her uncle visited.

However, the uncle took her back and gave her a

precious gift which she cherished so much and that was "Michael West Dictionary". That wonderful and precious gift led to the change of name and destiny of Ada for good. How did it happen? You may ask.

CHAPTER SEVEN

Ada's ingenuity unravelled when her name changed. Her other name connotes lateness. She was known for lateness to school during her primary school days. She was flogged, exposed to other forms of punishment and ridiculed by her classmates for being a habitual late comer. Her lateness to school was as a result of her engagement in petty trading such as frying groundnut before going to school. She developed the attitude of financial independence through hard work in her primary school days. That spirit of self-emancipation remained in her and helped her to sustain her vision. She would pick offences at the slightest provocation because her classmates especially the boys would sing derogatorily because of her lateness to school thus:

Angelina omee late
Ejema ejema omee late
Ayoma ayoma omee late

Ebe o n'ete pancake
O nwere ten percent10%,
20%, 30%, 40%, etc

In spite of her gentle disposition, she could fight to finish rather than allow her integrity to be trampled under feet. In fact, nobody could ever believe that she could dare the boys looking at her tender nature. Some boys in their class received groundnuts as reward by accepting to clear her portion of work during manual labour while she continued with her sales.

Inadvertently, as she was reading the Michael West Dictionary, her precious gift, she stumbled on the words that depict "strong, reliable, and dependable" she matched those words with an acronym she was using for her other names. That led to a change of name. So, it was from that time in her primary five when she discovered those words that changed her destiny.

Do you know the meaning of those words? Can you explain to me the rationale behind your choice of that name? The class teacher Mr. Emma queried Ada. "I know the meaning" she asserted. "Can you explain to me what those words mean?" Mr. Emma further probed her. "The words mean something used to hold a ship firmly to a place". "Yes" the teacher nodded. "But sir" Ada continued, "Can you imagine the size of a ship, the strength and the reliability of any instrument that could be used to hold it in a place? Can ordinary rope be used to tie a ship?" She paused and sought the answers to those questions from her teacher. "NO!" He affirmed. "Okay, that also depicts refuge or shelter" She added. "It therefore connotes that I am strong, reliable and dependable". "Wonderful!" the class teacher shouted. He could not hide his excitement over her outstanding boldness and intelligence. He commended her ingenuity and encouraged her to aspire higher in life.

CHAPTER EIGHT

The desire for greener pasture stirred Ada's sense of industry. She engaged in some manual labours that could yield money. That made her cousin to nickname her "buy and sell". Indeed she exhibited traits of greatness through hard-work and love for education. She hired people's farm for weeding and employed other people to do the work while she supervised, settled them afterward and made her own gain out of the business.

In the early 80's, Ada secured admission into one of the famous Girls' secondary schools within her locality (ObLondon). She distinguished herself both in academics and craft. She won many prizes as a result of her academic excellence in subjects like French and History. She became popular because of her new name which was novel to many people and the type of hair style she was known for. That trend continued until in her class three when their disciplinary master, Mr J.C spotted her out and invited her to the staff-room for interrogation. When she got to the staff-room, he called her by that new name and started raging in the staff-room by saying "Your name is ringing a bell in this school, tell us, are you a barber?" "No" Ada answered "But I know how to barb". He asked other questions while she was about to answer the questions, he reiterated "Your name is ringing a bell in this school oooh". After warning her about her hairstyle, he also discouraged her from barbing other students the same style of hair cut which he observed. Ada was among the few students that cleared their O'level examination in the school that year.

As a result of her mother's death, she forfeited her admission into College of Technology in the State Capital where she was offered Secretarial Administration. She will ever remember the last words of her mother before she gave up the ghost "My daughter, if somebody advises you to leave me on this sick bed and go to school, will you oblige? Please, take care of me and it will be well with you. As you take care of me, so shall your children take good care of you, whether I am alive or dead, do not allow anybody to take any of your siblings as house help" she concluded. Although Ada was robbed of that golden opportunity, she kept her dream and vision alive. Her journey for a greener pasture commenced a month after her mother's burial. One of her maternal cousins called Angel came and took her to the city. She introduced her to Chief Ugwumba, the Director in charge of city canteen who was in search of a good saleslady.

"Can I be given a portion or section of this business to manage while others take care of other sections?" Ada requested. "Yes you can" Chief Ugwumba obliged her. She was given initial capital of two hundred and fifty naira. Through her hard-work and transparent honesty, she made huge sales and the income that first month was a big surprise to Chief. To motivate her, he paid her forty naira instead of thirty naira that he was paying other. In the second month, she made more gain and he decided to pay her eighty naira as incentive.

About four months later, Chief Ugwumba leased the business outfit to somebody else who came with his own staff. Ada was able to secure another place on the recommendations of her Director. While working in the second place, she maintained her integrity. In fact, the owner of the place decried the huge loses he had suffered under those managing the business especially in the area of telephone calls without accounting for the proceeds, yet NITEL bills will accumulate on his name. Interestingly, she was faithful in rendering the account from the proceeds. This made the new Director, Owelle as he was popularly called to vow never to let go of her services. She kept accurate account of sales and phone calls differently. She generated much fund from the telephone business, by calling NITEL HQs for access codes whenever she had challenges connecting people outside the state. It was incredible for Oga Owelle, her new director to believe that such huge amount could be realised at the end of the month.

He decided to pay her twice what he was paying the previous workers. Whereas Ada was in control of the kitchen and telephone calls, Tina another saleslady was in charge of the drinks. The unfortunate thing about Tina was that, though she was pretty-looking, she wasn't trustworthy. On one occasion, Tina was asked to take care of the kitchen while she left for the market; Tina made away with some rice from the bag in the kitchen. Also, she tampered with the pot of pepper soup. As if nobody will find out, she carefully buried the rice behind the refrigerator.

As meticulous as she was, when she came in, by instinct went straight to that fridge; saw the rice and without uttering any word quietly carried that rice. She waited for the moment Tina would raise an alarm. Eventually, about the time Tina wanted to go, she discovered that the rice was no longer where she kept it. She started soliloquising, making cynical comments like "ITK the only I Too Know in the whole world". Ada didn't respond to such side talks rather reported the matter to their neighbour.

Immediately, the neighbour came, "Tina why are you soliloquizing?" he queried. But she ignored him. "Desist from such petty habits Tina it will lead you nowhere" he concluded and left. Tina resorted to singing derogatory songs. Later, Ada reported the case officially to their Director who, after hearing from both parties, paid Tina off. "You must look for someone else who is honest, compactable and can work with you soon" Oga Owelle told her. That she did without much ado. She enjoyed her stay with the new person; as the name of that place actually implied freedom palace until Chief Ugwumba, her former Director came looking for her.

CHAPTER NINE

One good turn deserves another is a true to life saying. Ada unknowingly endeared herself to Sir Godson, the Landlord who was a retired principal. Each time he came from the village asking for house rent, she would quickly pay him instead of turning him down considering the distance and old age. She never knew the extent the Landlord valued her deeds of kindness and respect for old age, until when an unscrupulous individual went to buy his heart by trying to offer him more money in terms of rent in order to dispossess her. But the Landlord rejected the offer and revealed it to her.

"Please, come and take over the management of City Canteen, I want to join politics, not only that the people running it are full of creative accounting" Chief Ugwumba persuaded Ada. She was halting in-between opinions because she has settled for her new place of work and has no reason to disappoint Oga Owelle. But when she weighed the options with due consultations; she discovered that Chief Ugwumba's offer was the best. That unprecedented favour was to reciprocate her hard-work and faithfulness when she was serving him. "I don't have silver or gold to give you for your faithful services, please come and take this business and pay me a token" Chief Ugwumba concluded. Her uncle assisted her financially to secure and gain ownership of that venture.

Ada quickly arranged and brought two of her siblings Ikem and Nnedinma to town. She enrolled Ikem in JSS 1 while Nnedinma enrolled into primary four. In addition to her sales boys and girls, her siblings were also helping in the business after school. For Ada, life wasn't a bed of roses; even roses have thorns.

She lost some prospective suitors because some of them thought that her siblings would pose a serious responsibility on them. In fact, one of the whimsical suitors stated categorically; "I wish you are from a wealthy family and have a university education otherwise my brother's wives will use you as a maid". That statement spurred her interest to further her education.

The course of nature made her to become mother

surrogate to her younger siblings. She didn't allow her past to negatively influence her present or the future. She was more dogged, resolute and determined to make it in life God willing.

With a good O' level certificate, it was possible for Ada to enrol for the Nigeria Certificate in Education (NCE) in one of the best Colleges of Education in the country. After obtaining the NCE, she further enrolled for degree programme in one of the prestigious university in the country.

Truly, education is a gateway to a brighter future and a ladder to social mobility. As soon as Ada entered the tertiary institution, suitors started coming again both those with real intentions and the fake ones. At that point, she was careful never to fall prey in the hands of whimsical suitors. She was the person making the choice and no longer the other way round. She remained grateful to all the people who gave her wise counsels. Eventually, Ada got married and settled down with her heart throb.

Contrary to man's ideology and popular opinion, she got married and was blessed with male and female children; in addition she got her first degree. To actualise her dream, her husband gave her the ticket to go for more degrees. She effectively combined education and child bearing with God on her side.

CHAPTER TEN

"Show me your friend and I will tell you who you are". This is an age long saying that is true to life. Ada would always reminiscence over her uncle's piece of advice which served as a checklist and helped to build her confidence in choosing her confidence in choosing her friends.

One day, Ada and her friends Onyii visited her uncle from the hostel while in the University. "Is this your friend?" Her uncle asked. Yes uncle, Ada replied.

"Well, I want to remind you of some realities about life, the uncle began. "Remember, as you make your bed so you will lie on it". Do you know that? Ada chorused, "Yes uncle". Again do you also know that evil communication corrupts good manners? She answered in affirmation.

Okay, listen Now that you are in the university, if you keep one good friend, you may not have any problem, but if you keep one hundred friends, so shall your problems be multiplied. Therefore, use your tongue to count your teeth, uncle Ehis concluded.

Indeed, it's all about a turning point in the history of Ada. She became a graduate of one of the famous Universities in the country. Thereafter, she secured her first job with the State Universal Basic Education Board. She experienced a dramatic change as a result of spiritual transformation after her encounter with the grace of God. Those who knew her couldn't believe that she could afford to abandon the beauty and pleasures of this world. Some people were asking "How did it happen?"

After giving birth to her fourth son, the mother in-law who was overwhelmed with joy exclaimed; "My daughter, you have made me a proud grandma. I would not have asked for a better daughter in-law than you. I have seen someone that will not only take care of you, but also me. You have given us a military squad. I am so grateful to God", she danced this way and that way, moving her body to the surprise of her observers.

"Mama, so you can still dance this way? We thought age has overtaken you".

"Ah! Ah! My children, haven't you heard that a woman does not grow old in a song she is skillful in? My age cannot be a barrier. Even at my oldest age, I will still prove it".

"Mama, are you sure?" her son asked jokingly. "Yes, my son. Have you joined the gang of Thomases? Have you forgotten how I won several awards with my skill at women meetings? You are yet to see something" "Of course not, Mama you know I have not and can't, I trust you fulltime".

The end of her dancing show attracted applause from people around. Actually, Ada's mother in-law exhibited her skills at St. Mary's Hospital. Her action instantly made the doctor in-charge her fan. "Congratulations on the safe delivery of your daughter in-law Ma. I must say that dance respects no age. You really impressed me. Couldn't believe you can still dance this way. May God keep and prolong your life Ma" said the Doctor. "Amen!!" the peoples shouted to his prayer. As soon as he was done, he quickly moved to attend to other vital issues. When he was almost out of sight, Little Bright cried in protest of his departure. His voice attracted a voice which interpreted it as displeasure because of her nationality, Nigerian.

"Chai, cry no more little angel. It's just the fault of our leaders and indirectly ours, indirectly because we gave them mandate. I know you are not pleased, but please, cry no more. With God on our side, it shall be well. You look like your mother and grandmother little angel, so handsome and lovely." The stranger said.

At first, when the stranger referred to the cry of a little boy as a displeasure and unhappiness, her grandmother made protest. Amidst all the words of the stranger, the last two statements strengthened her. They brightened her face with joy. She was happy to be addressed as a beautiful woman even at old age.

While she was preparing to leave the hospital after seven days, because the doctor was waiting for her baby's jaundice to clear, Ada had a nerve-racking dream that brought about a positive change in her. In that dream, two men were after her life. She ran and ran to the point that she was panting for breath. As she was running for safety in a lonely path, she felt that those men were no longer pursuing her as they were out of sight. Then she began to walk, lo and behold, suddenly an unknown animal from nowhere jumped out from a ditch and bit her fingers. While her fingers were in that animal's mouth, she was gripped with fear as she struggled to free her hand, guess what? Her head started turning in dizziness as if a recap of that dream and all that she passed through. Her eye balls were as if they wanted to pull out from their sockets. She felt serious headache and palpitations. As soon as the doctor entered the ward early that morning, he went straight to Ada's bed only to observe that she was dying by instalment. Immediately, the doctor asked the nurses to rush her to his office. He called for her file.

After going through the file, he queried the source of the raised blood pressure (B.P). According to the doctor, Ada had her three other children in that hospital without a trace of BP case for the past eight years. "Madam, did you ever pray after that dream?" The doctor further probed her not satisfied with the strange happenings. "I prayed according to my strength" she responded. "No!!" The doctor retorted. "This is neither a case of praying according to your strength nor a medical case. Do you know of any prayer warrior?" he continued. "Please hurry up because I am going to discharge you right away so that you can go and look for those who are strong in prayer. I can't prescribe any B.P drug for you" he concluded.

Eventually, Nnedinma who was taking care of her in the hospital, rallied for a vehicle that took them home. When Ada got home that day, friends and neighbours who came around could not believe what they saw because of her state of health. She was weak because she has not been eating food rather was demanding for anything liquid. She was restless, unconscious and lost sleep whenever she had a flashback of the nightmare. She would start melting like a cube of sugar that comes in contact with water. She became afraid of death and as such was dying gradually. One early morning, she remembered a certain man of God who was loved by children. Afterwards, she scribbled something for the man of God and sent her sister and her first son who was tender in age, inviting him to come urgently.

When he came about 9am, he started apologizing for coming late "My sister I am sorry for coming a little bit late… I had to take my wife to her office" " it's okay sir" she replied him with a smile. "So how are you? What's the matter?" he enquired. When she gave a recap of what happened, he made light of the situation and challenged her to have faith. Before he prayed, he read two portions of the scripture, "For as many that received Him, to them He gave the power to become the sons of God even to them that believed on His name" and about the conversion of Cornelius. He told her emphatically "If you have faith in God based on these scriptures I have read to you, you shall be healed". At that point, she was gazing at him as if he had life in his hands. "Now confess your sins and ask God for forgiveness" he urged her. Ada confessed all her sins, asked for forgiveness and promised to serve God forever if she survived the ordeal. Immediately, he laid his hand on her head and prayed for her. After the prayers, she testified "I felt something like a pinch of ice on my head while the prayer was on going". He prayed the second time thanking God for a confirmation of that miracle of healing. The night following, she requested for food. She had another dream that same night. She was asked to read in a scroll written in different languages. She could not read in those languages until she saw the one written in English language "I am free", she read out with excitement and jumped up only to discover that it was in a dream.

She prayed as she could, slept and had a second dream that same night where she was asked to read a portion in the book of life. She could not find one handy, so while she was searching for one, she woke up and found that it was a dream. In the morning a Nurse came to see her. So, when she remembered those dreams, she narrated them to the Nurse who gave her their interpretations. She became convinced and satisfied. She was invited to fellowship with the Scripture Union (SU) nearest to her, she honoured the invitation. She developed a burning desire to know and to serve God more and more. After sharing the testimony of her salvation in the fellowship, she was prayed for.

From that day, members of SU family were visiting her regularly, praying and encouraging her to continue in the faith.

One Sunday morning, her sister in-law came visiting from Enyimba city. While her sister in-law prepared for church service, Ada on her own volition followed her to their church and asked her children to go to their own church. On that fateful day, a miracle took place on the altar which she claimed was for her conviction. She would ever remember the message "Breaking the barriers in your personal and family life"

Point 1: Causes of barriers, 2: Consequences of barriers, 3: Solutions to barriers

It was at point 3, that a tall, well-dressed young man ran from one corner of the church towards the pastor on the altar to attack him but he was rolled away by a divine power like a ball. Three times on the wall, he started bleeding and the ushers rushed him away. It was after the service that he confessed, "I was ona deadly mission from Raba to Ibam, and how I found myself in this church is a mystery to me".

CHAPTER ELEVEN

To maintain a conscience free from guilt after due counselling, Ada embarked upon restitutions. "Go ahead and do it, restitution will bring restoration" her regional pastor advised her.

First, she returned all the illegal items in her possession to their rightful owners. Second, concerning the wrong or false age declaration she was using, no one would have imagined the aftermath when her name was captured and she was summoned at NUT Secretariat.

The irony of the whole situation was that she put the correct age declaration without withdrawing the wrong one from her file at the Local Government Education Authority (LGEA). The Head master of her school, Sir Ozichi became red. "Why should her name be shortlisted since she has no TTC? He queried. "Let me go and find out from the LGEA, the Headmaster concluded. Although, the government was trying to fish out those who have fake TTC certificate, it was discovered that Ada was summoned because she had two age certificates. Her colleagues were jeering at her "Are you the only christian going to heaven?" don't you know that one can operate with official age certificate and the birth certificate notwithstanding? "Weep for yourself, I am not afraid, I am convinced that they will neither take my certificate nor my salvation if I am fired" she responded. So she went to NUT Secretariat on the D-day. Her case was the first to be addressed. When the podium was set, the chairman of the panel, Barr. Chimdi Egbula announced Ada's name and she was taken to the podium. Her case was read and the Lawyer asked her: "Are you Ada? She answered in affirmation "Yes sir!". The Lawyer began "We are sorry to summon you because you are not a TTC candidate, but we saw two age certificates in your file". He said, now tell us out of these two age declaration/certificates, which one would you want us to take and which one to disregard? She started by pleading guilty "I did that in ignorance, please forgive me". In a twinkling of an eye, she narrated how she came to know the Lord and how the Lord has spoken to her to make right every wrong. The Lawyer shouted, Madam! Do you know what you are saying? Do you want to go early? And do you want to give the government seven years? She answered in affirmation "YES SIR!!" The lawyer was flabbergasted. "Which church do you attend?" Before she could finish saying "Deeper--- Immediately, he held her hand and introduced her to the congress saying "Look at a christian in deed..." There was jubilation in the house contrary to her colleague's expectations.

After a year, the SUBEB officials conducted a promotion exercise in her LGEA. She was given double promotion from Grade level 08 to 10 due to the recommendations of that panel following that restitution. Some people testified that actually it pays to be honest.

Ada's new life experience was as glaring as that of Saint Paul. Like Saul, She was zealous and playing religion without righteousness. The issue of new-birth never occurred to her until that fateful day.

To confirm her healing, she received a wonderful revelation and that spurred her to serve God without hypocrisy. But, her unfeigned love and devotion to God attracted persecution from her colleagues in her place of work. That was evident in signing the attendance register. Ada would come to school early to conduct the morning assembly, so those that came late find it difficult to sign the wrong time. That became a source of persecution. But, she was loved by all those who cherish the truth especially the Head mistress, Mrs. Mgboji who held her in high esteem due to her powerful communication skill and transparent honesty.

Consequently, the H/M of the school with the approval of Sir Chris, the Education Secretary encouraged her to go for her Master's degree programme. She ceased the opportunity because their school has morning and afternoon shifts. So, it was possible for her to quickly run her Master's degree programme in one of the nearby Universities on part time basis. Their lecture days were Friday evenings and Saturdays because those involved in the programme were all working in one parastatal or the other. Eventually, she obtained her Master's degree and thereafter began to crave for a greener pasture.

CHAPTER TWELVE

Prior to Ada's the divine relocation, Buchi her hubby had hitches in his business. The first encounter was during the Sharia palavar in the Northern part of the country. He lost all in the course of Sharia except his life. He relocated to Enyimba city in the South-East. He started doing well again with the support of his younger brother in Italy. In fact, it was an act of providence that his younger brother responded promptly because nobody thought it could have been possible because according to their elder brother residing in Lag, no one has been able to communicate with the younger brother for quite a long time. It was not long, when an unscrupulous young man called Kingsley, an old friend of Buchi met him in Enyimba city. "Hello Buchi what are you doing here?" "I am residing here since after the Sharia case" replied Buchi. "What are you doing here too? Buchi asked. Furthermore, Kingsley queried "Where do you buy your goods?" "Cotonou and Togo" Buchi replied.

"Come and see my warehouse, you may not need to travel out to buy because I will not only subsidize the prizes for you as an old friend, but regularly supply your needs" Kingsley asserted.

According to Buchi, he went and saw that it was exactly what he was travelling to Cotonou or Togo to buy that his friend has brought to town. After due negotiation, He was asked to pay and go and get a bus that will convey his goods to his shop. Buchi ran to the shop, collected all his money, collected from three people also. After payment, he went to get a bus that will carry the goods to his shop.

Unfortunately, before he could get a bus, and come back, the hoodlums had made away with the goods. Buchi wanted to kill himself because it involved other people's money. But through proper counselling, he surrendered his life to Christ. He relocated to the village as a result of that hitch.

Nevertheless, the people whose monies were involved traced him to their village but Ada's wisdom prevailed. She spoke softly and pleaded with the men to bear with her husband rather they should hold her responsible. She expressed her optimism thus "If I defend my Masters' Thesis and get a better job, I will settle the indebtedness". They remained mute were after hearing from her. She probed them further to speak their mind concerning her request. "You have said it" they stood up and left. Little did Ada know that her positive confession has received divine approval.

It was not long, she defended her thesis successfully and the next year ushered into divine repositioning. Ada visited her mentor in the campus, who took her to the Dean of their faculty, the man God used to re-write her history. Her mentor pleaded with the Dean to consider Ada's plight "Please my Dean give her the hook to fish and not the fish itself". In a twinkling of an eye, she has narrated her ordeal which made the Dean to melt. Meanwhile, the Dean was sharing his testimony with his colleague in his office on how a particular minister has been praying for him over the phone and it has been working for him even though he has not seen him physically. At that point, Ada caught in and said "Sir, I will help you the more, if you have a prayer request bring".

The man was surprised at her audacity but complied immediately without asking questions. Quickly, he suspended the discussion with his colleague, turned and wrote something enveloped it and handed it over to her. She ran back to her mentor's office and showed her the money he gave her for transport. Her mentor came back to thank him and reiterated "I prefer giving her the hook to giving her the fish". That day, she went home happy and rejoicing that something new has started in her life. She remembered one of the church programmes held the previous year captioned "Divine Repositioning for a Desirable Life".

The thought about that programme alone helped to fuel her aspiration. She took that prayer request as it was in an envelope to her Regional Pastor on a counselling day. He opened the envelope and saw one thousand naira note. He gave it back to Ada to return to the man, "We don't sell prayers" the pastor said. He read out the three points in the request and prayed while she knelt down. After the day, she went home satisfied, believing that answer has come already. She gave that one thousand naira note to S.U offering. Thereafter, she started sending Bible references to the man God used to reposition her.

It was not long, he called and said; "Sister, God has answered two of those requests, what can I do for you? Do you have higher degrees – like Masters? If yes, please bring it as well as your other documents. She did not hesitate in doing that. The next year, he was the first person to give Ada new year message "Sister, God will give you uncommon miracle for uncommon testimony this year".

She believed God for the best while serving the Lord unreservedly. Another revelation was that of crossing the River Jordan. It was not long, she was called for an interview. Thereafter, her name was shortlisted but wrongly written. That became another battle. Were it not for the mercies of God, she would have lost the chance but, the man would always call and say "Sister please continue to pray, there is a battle here and the heat is much". The trend continued till the day she was called for her appointment letter. On getting there, the woman issuing the appointment letter queried her "Are you the person the Dean was disturbing us for?" She posed some questions and Ada readily provided their answers. She threw the appointment letter at her and sighed annoyingly.

She took the appointment letter to the Dean and narrated her encounter with the woman that gave her the appointment letter. The Dean in turn, took time to narrate his own ordeal. How the management gave him options either to choose the two other candidates or Ada. "Give me this one and council the other two" the Dean demanded.

Although she was not properly placed, she humbled herself while serving in that lowly domain. Two years later, she was transferred for proper placement in the institution. The same year, she was among the highly favoured, a scholarship was granted for a Doctoral Degree programme in one of the Federal Universities in the country. She rounded off her Ph.D programme within a record time.

Indeed, Ada may not be a millionaire but spiritually she is a millionaire. In the field of academics, she could be reckoned as a giant. An erudite scholar, a silent achiever, self-made with God on her side. "It is not of him that willeth neither of him that runneth but of God that showeth mercy" How can one explain this uncommon miracle of mercy? Those who despised Ada, can now praise God on her behalf. As one Igbo adage says; *"Ehi n'enweghi odu, chi ya n'achuru ya ijiji"* Truly, "God keeps away flies from the tail-less cow".

CHAPTER THIRTEEN

RIDDLES ABOUT LIFE ACCORDING TO STEVE JOBS

You can employ someone to drive
The car for you,
Make money for you.
But nobody can die for you and
No one else can live your life for you
Material things lost could be found,
But there is one thing that can
Never be found when it is lost:
"LIFE"

When a person goes into the operation room,
He will realize that there is only one book
That he has yet to finish reading;
"The Book of life"
Whichever stage in life
We are at right now,
With time, we will face the day
When the curtain comes down

Treasure love for your family,
Love for your spouse,
Love for your friends...
Treat yourself well.
Cherish others
As we grow older and hence wiser,
We slowly realize that...
Wearing a N500.00 or N1m wrist watch,
They both tell the same time...
Whether we carry a N1m or N2 handbag;
It doesn't matter much
The amount of money inside
Is still the same.

Whether we drive the most expensive or the
cheapest car;
The road and distance remain the same,
And will get to the same destination.

Whether the house we live in is 300 or 3000 sq.ft;
Loneliness is the same
You will realize,
Your true inner happiness
Does not come from
The material things of this world.

Whether you fly first class or economy class,
If the plane goes down
You go down with it...
Therefore ... I hope you realize
When you have class mates,
Buddies and old friends,
Brothers and sisters,
Who you chat with, laugh with,
Talk with, have sing songs with,
Talk about north-south-east-west
Or heaven and earth
That is true happiness!!

FIVE UNDENIABLE FACTS OF LIFE:

1. Don't educate your children to be rich.
   Educate them to be happy
   So when they grow up, they will know the value of things,
   Not the price.

2. Best awarded words in London...
   "Eat your food as your medicines.
   Otherwise, you have to eat medicine as your food".

3. The ones who love you will never leave you for another because
   Even if there are 1000 reasons to give up, he or she will find one reason to hold on.

4. There is a big difference between a human being and being human.
   Only a few really understand it.

5. You are loved when you are born.
   You will be loved when you die.

In between, you have to manage!

Note: If you just want to walk fast,
      Walk alone!
      But if you want to walk far,
      Walk together

Six Best Doctors in the world...
1. Sunlight
2. Rest
3. Exercise
4. Diet
5. Self-confidence and
6. Good Friends

Maintain them in all stages of life and enjoy a healthy life.

God loves you!

GLOSSARY

Ada	The first daughter
Nma	Beauty
Umualaoma	The name of a town
Pa	The short form of Papa
Akuma	The name of a town
The Aro's	The people that migrated from a town called Arochukwu (Aro's in diaspora)
"Kamalu Ozuzu"	The name of a diety people use for cursing.
Nwatawelie Ukwu elu	Asking the child to double her steps and walk faster

"Akwa gi sim
Welieukwu m elu"

You asked me to raise my legs up.

Kai kai

The name of a local dry gin or hot drink.

"Unu dum"

All of you

Uya

The name of a Town (Uya market)

Eze Muo

The chief of the spirits

Oji

Iron digger

"Erontuochi"

A Dermanent smiling face

Kpolaa moo

A cry to take me back home

Angelina omee late
Ejema ejema omee late

Ayoma ayoma omee late
Ebe o n'ete pancake
O nwere 10%, 20%, 30%, 40% etc

A derogatory song for a habitual late comer, whether when going or coming back as a result of pancake.

Enyimba	A name of a town
Owelle	A chieftaincy title
ITK	I Too Know
Chai	An exclamation
NUT	Nigerian Union Of Teachers
TTC	Teachers Training College
NCE	Nigerian Certificate in Education

"Ehi enwe odu, chi ya n'achuru ya ijiji" meaning that " God keeps flies away from the tail-less cow".

Destiny can be delayed but it cannot be denied. Dare like Daniel, Remain Focused!!!

ABOUT THE AUTHOR

Dr. (Mrs) Ngozi Anchor-Lee Okoro (Nee Ugorji) hails from Okwu Umuoma Nekede Owerri West by birth and Eluama Owerre-Ebeiri in Orlu LGA by marriage. She holds a Nigeria Certificate in Education (NCE) English/Literature, Alvan Ikoku Fedral College of Education Owerri, B.A.Ed English, University of Nigeria Nsukka, Masters of Arts, English Language, Imo state University, Owerri and Ph.D English Language, University Uyo. She is currently a Senior Lecturer in the Department of Primary Education, Alvan Ikoku Federal College of Education. She is a member of many Professional Associations, including Colleges of Education Academic Staff Union (COEASU), English Language Teachers Association of Nigeria (ELTAN), Reading Association on Nigeria (RAN), Organization of Early Childhood Education (OMEP), and National Association of Childhood Motivators (NACM) among others. Dr. Anchor-Lee has Published extensively particularly in reputable Peer reviewed journals, attended and presented paper at national and international conferences.

The author tells her story in an interesting way drawing from her personal experiences and realities of the society to weave a story that is engaging and educative especially for the girl child on how to overcome the deeply entrenched obstacles that create invisible chasm in our society. Characters were drawn from a composite of real-life people who had participated in real life events that had historical significance to the author.

Dr. (Mrs) A.C Izuagba.